To Norma &
Aomar –

With very best wishes
from Hotdog & me!

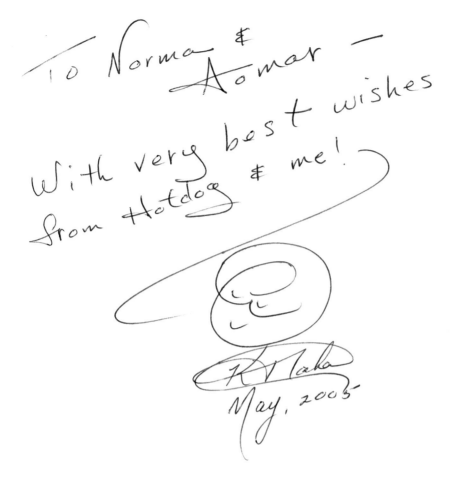

May, 2005

Hotdog on TV

Karen T. Taha ★ *pictures by* Hideko Takahashi

DIAL BOOKS FOR YOUNG READERS
New York

To Sarah Elizabeth Taha,
with loads of love
—K. T. T.

To my family and Chonkey
—H. T.

The artist gives thanks to B. J. Paine of King TV
for a great station tour.

Published by Dial Books for Young Readers
A division of Penguin Young Readers Group
345 Hudson Street • New York, New York 10014
Text copyright © 2005 by Karen T. Taha
Pictures copyright © 2005 by Hideko Takahashi
All rights reserved
Designed by Jasmin Rubero
Manufactured in China on acid-free paper
The Dial Easy-to-Read logo is a registered trademark of
Dial Books for Young Readers,
a division of Penguin Young Readers Group ® TM 1,162,718.

1   3   5   7   9   10   8   6   4   2

Library of Congress Cataloging-in-Publication Data
Taha, Karen T.
Hotdog on TV / Karen T. Taha ; pictures by Hideko Takahashi.
p.   cm.
Summary: A small brown dog auditions for a television commercial.
ISBN 0-8037-2933-2
[1. Dogs—Fiction. 2. Television advertising—Fiction.]
I. Takahashi, Hideko, ill. II. Title.
PZ7.T1288Ho 2005   [E]—dc21   2003002356
Reading Level 2.1

The art was created using acrylics.

Contents

Hotdog, Ice Cream, and TV

Hotdog is lonely in the animal shelter.
When Mr. Beans comes to the shelter,
Hotdog runs around his legs
and licks him all over.
Then Mr. Beans takes Hotdog home
to Mrs. Beans.

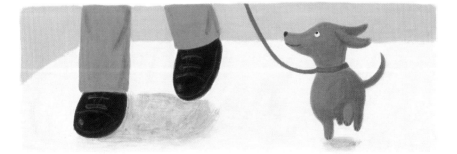

And now . . .

Mrs. Beans gives Hotdog ice cream.

His tongue goes *lickity-lick!*

After Hotdog eats his ice cream,

he takes a nap under the TV.

One day, as Hotdog is napping,
Mr. Beans says, "Wake up, Hotdog!"
He points at the television.
"They are looking for a dog
to be on TV."

Hotdog opens his eyes.
TV dogs have long legs and run fast,
he thinks. I'm just a little brown dog
with short legs and a hot-dog body.

"They want a dog to eat
Doggy Yums Dog Food on TV,"
Mr. Beans says.

Hotdog thumps his tail on the floor.
Hey! I can do that!
Then there will be a dog on TV
who looks like me—ME!

"They want a dog who is happy and healthy,"
says Mr. Beans.

"Hotdog is happy," says Mrs. Beans.

"He is healthy too," says Mr. Beans.

"Ah-choo!" Hotdog sneezes.
"Except for his allergies,"
   says Mr. Beans.

"Let's go to the TV studio!"
   says Mrs. Beans.

Hotdog jumps in Mrs. Beans's taxi.
As they drive to the TV studio,
Hotdog's ears go *flappity-flap.*
His heart thumps *bumpity-bump.*
"I'm going to be on TV!" barks Hotdog.

At the TV studio Hotdog jumps out of
Mrs. Beans's taxi.
He sees all sorts of dogs.
He sees his friends Fifi and Hans.
They want to be on TV too.

Hotdog follows Fifi and Hans
into the waiting room.
Dogs go in and dogs come out.
Soon there are only three left—
Fifi, Hans, and Hotdog.

"They want a pretty dog
to eat Doggy Yums on TV,"
Fifi's owner tells Mrs. Beans.
"Fifi is very pretty," says Mrs. Beans.

"They want a strong dog
to eat Doggy Yums on TV,"
Hans's owner tells Mr. Beans.
"Hans is big and strong,"
says Mr. Beans.

I'm not pretty or big or strong,
Hotdog thinks.
I'm a short brown dog who sneezes.
Hotdog starts to feel like a flat tire
on Mrs. Beans's taxi.
"S-s-s-s-s," he sighs.

"They also want a very good eater,"
says Mrs. Beans.

Hotdog sits up.

I am a VERY good eater! he thinks.

I CAN be on TV!

Finally, the door opens.

A man calls out, "You three next."

Hotdog Meets the Director

Hotdog watches a tall man walk
back and forth.
He watches a small boy walk
behind him.

The boy is licking an ice cream cone.
Hotdog sees the cone dripping
pink polka dots on the floor.
Drippity-drip goes the ice cream.
Yummm, thinks Hotdog.

"That man is the director,"
Mrs. Beans whispers.
"He will choose which dog
gets to be on TV."
Fifi and Hans sit up straight and tall.

Hotdog sits up too,
but he is still not tall.
"Oof!"
The director trips over Hotdog.
He falls into Mr. Beans's lap.
"Ruff-ruff!" barks Hotdog.

The little boy laughs so hard,
he drops his ice cream cone.
It makes a pink puddle on the floor.

The director points at Hotdog.

"Who is that?" he asks.

"That is Hotdog," Mrs. Beans says.

"He is a very good eater."

Hotdog looks up at the director.

He looks down at the pink puddle.

He drools on the director's shoes.

24

"Uh, the other dogs are Fifi and Hans,"
Mr. Beans says quickly.
He hopes the director
won't look at his shoes.
Fifi wags her fluffy white tail.
"Yip-yip!" she says.
Hans puffs out his big strong chest.
"Woof-woof!" he says.
Hotdog scoots closer
to the pink ice cream puddle.
"Mmmm-yum!" says his tummy.

The Cameras Roll

The director climbs into his tall chair.
"Roll the cameras!" he says.
Fifi runs to her bowl of Doggy Yums.
She eats the Doggy Yums one by one—
munchity-munch.

Hans runs to his bowl of Doggy Yums.
He eats the Doggy Yums in one big gulp—
chomp!

Hotdog runs to the pink puddle.
He licks the ice cream—*slurpity-slurp!*

But Hotdog's feet will not stay still
on the slippery floor.
Hotdog slides. Hotdog spins.
His feet go *slippity-slam*
into his bowl of Doggy Yums.

Doggy Yums fly all over!

"Oo-woo-woo!" Hotdog howls.

The little boy laughs and laughs.

"Cut the cameras!" the director yells.

"Good job," the director says to Fifi.

"Good job," the director says to Hans.

"B-u-r-p," says Hotdog.
He licks his sticky paws.

"Which dog do you like best?"
the director asks the boy.
"That one, Daddy!" Rex says.
He is pointing to Hotdog!

The director nods. "You are right.
He will make people smile.
They will want to buy Doggy Yums."
"It's true," says Mrs. Beans.
"Hotdog makes us smile every day."

Hotdog will be on TV!
He runs around the room,
eating all the Doggy Yums.
Crunchity-crunch.
But suddenly . . .

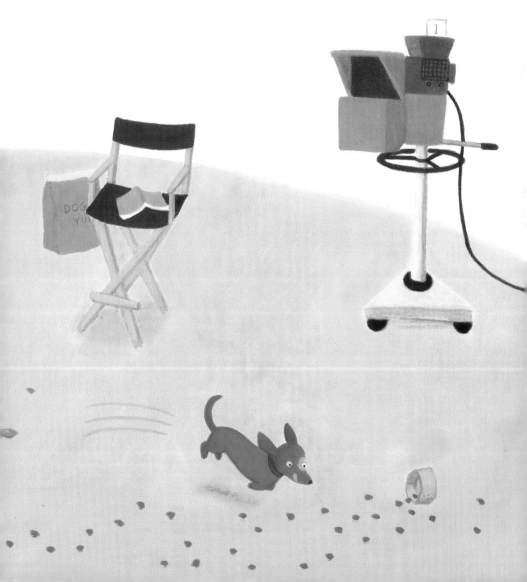

"Ah-choo!" Hotdog sneezes.

"Ah-choo! Ah-choo!"

Hotdog sneezes and sneezes.

"Oh, no!" says Mr. Beans.

"Hotdog is allergic to Doggy Yums."

Hotdog's ears droop.

He won't be on TV after all.

"You are still a very good eater,"

says Mrs. Beans.

She carries Hotdog to her taxi.

Hotdog sleeps on Mr. Beans's lap
on the drive home.
Then he curls up under the television.
"Maybe someday you will be on TV,"
Mr. Beans tells Hotdog.
"For now, you will just be under it.
But we love you just the same."

The phone rings.

"Hello?" says Mrs. Beans.

"Really?" says Mrs. Beans.

She holds the phone out
so Mr. Beans and Hotdog can hear.

"I'm sorry Hotdog cannot eat
Doggy Yums Dog Food," the director says.

"But we are making a new product—
Doggy Yums Ice Cream!
It will have five different flavors.
We will find one
that will not make Hotdog sneeze!"

"What do you think about that, Hotdog?"
asks Mrs. Beans.

Hotdog thumps his tail.

Whumpity-whump!

A little brown dog with
short legs and a hot-dog body
WILL be on TV!

That night, Hotdog dreams of ice cream.
Pink, white, yellow, green,
and brown—just like him.
Lickity-lickity-lick.